A Soul Seen

A Paranormal Romance

Lola B. Marie

Book Cover by Gurcheva Evgeniia.

Edited by Jaquelyn Vale, @_shewhoedits_ on Instagram.

For inquiries please contact: lola.b.marie.author@gmail.com.

1st edition 2025

Contents

To everyone who has a crazy idea that would make a great book but you don't think you can do it. Let me tell you…you can!

And to the best friends who keep a straight face when, "Remind me to tell you about my ghost porn idea," gets whispered in your ear during a public tour. You're the real heroes.

Note From the Author

TRIGGER WARNINGS

A Soul Seen is a paranormal romance. This book is intended for adult readers (18+), as it contains explicit language and detailed sexual scenes.

If any of the following make you uncomfortable, please proceed with caution or consider choosing a different book. Your mental health matters.

This list <u>WILL</u> contain spoilers for the story.

-Explicit Language

-Explicit Sexual Scenes

-Death

-Depression

-Suicide

If you or someone you know is contemplating suicide, please call the National Suicide Prevention Lifeline at 1-800-273-TALK (8255) or go online to 988lifeline.org.

Prologue

1886

The wind surged as he settled on the hotel's slanted roof. As a stonemason, he was used to working on high gables and barely gave it a second thought. He closed his eyes, taking in the smell of the crisp air blowing through the forest surrounding the hotel. A storm was coming.

"Patrick! She's back," John hollered from across the ridge, pulling him out of the moment. But for Clara, the distraction was worth it. She was a new maid, and he was interested. He maneuvered his way closer to John to see if he could catch her attention.

"Clara!" he yelled, but she didn't look up. She was quickly walking towards the covered entrance of the hotel. Concerned he would miss his chance before she went under that awning, he crouched down, leaning slightly over the edge.

"Clara!" This time she looked up and offered him a shy smile. Satisfied that he had her attention, he raised his hand to wave but lost his balance as a large gust of wind blew over the rooftop. Before he could regain his footing, he was falling. Clara's shy smile disappeared, only to be replaced with a look of terror. Then everything went black.

Chapter One

Present Day

"And that brings us back to your room. The most haunted room in the hotel and the most requested. This room is haunted by Patrick, our flirty ghost. He is said to have died in the late 1800s. He was a young stonemason who fell off the roof of the hotel while trying to get the attention of a young woman. Guests who stay in this room report their hair being gently tugged, the feeling of someone caressing their shoulder—sometimes even light laughter. This room is popular for bachelorette parties and girls' weekends. Everyone wants to get Patrick's attention." The tour guide pauses with an exaggerated wink.

Why am I here? Why did I agree to this ridiculous trip?

The other women around me are tipsy after sipping—*who are we kidding...downing*—their grapefruit mimosas as we walked through the Lunar Hotel on their ghost tour. I don't drink, but even if I did, grapefruit mimosas do not sound appealing. Layla paired the pink grapefruit juice with a sparkling pink Moscato. Yeah, pink is the theme here. Very original for a bachelorette party. I am the only one not decked out in penis-shaped accessories and bright pink costume jewelry.

"Emery! Don't look so perturbed! Patrick won't give you any attention with your face downturned like that!" Layla laughs and pinches my cheeks, attempting to form my face into a smile. My baby sister is getting married, and I've never seen her so happy. Sometimes it still surprises me how different we turned out. As kids, the differences weren't so glaring. But time and depression make excellent dividers in any relationship. Baby Sis got a healthy brain. Me, not so much. And since Layla has that naturally sunny disposition about everything, she can't understand me when even the medication doesn't hold off the inevitable dips in serotonin.

"Don't worry, Layla. I am *living* for Patrick's attention right now," I respond sarcastically. But I force my face into the best fake smile I can muster. This is about her, and the least I can do is play along. It seems to appease her because she turns from me and starts chittering with her best friend, Cassidy, about all the salacious things ghostly Patrick must have witnessed in this room over the years.

"Alright, ladies. This is where I leave you. I hope you enjoyed the tour. Please don't forget to take the survey that will be emailed to you shortly. Any feedback helps!" The tour guide—*I can't for the life of me remember her name* —gives us a little wave as she takes off down the dim hallway. Layla pulls her room key out of the beaded clutch she carries and lets everyone into the room.

It's a decent-sized suite. As we enter, there is a small kitchenette to the right and an open sitting area in the middle of the room with a pull-out couch. Past the kitchenette is a separate bedroom with two queen beds and the bathroom.

There are five of us in the party. I graciously offer to take the couch so the other four can share the beds. It's going to be difficult enough for me to sleep here, let alone if I had to share a bed with someone, even if it was my sister. My ever-churning thoughts don't shut off unless I am in the prime sleeping environment: fan or white noise, 69-72 degrees, thick blanket, and multiple pillows. I also have a prescription for sleeping pills, but I try not to take those, as they make me groggy the next morning. Hence the cultivated sleeping environment. So, yeah, hotel rooms are not usually conducive to picky sleepers like me, and I didn't feel like toting all my stuff on this trip. I can manage for one night.

Everyone piles into the sitting area, where Cassidy starts setting out the alcohol and mixers she brought. She happily took on the responsibility of planning this trip, which should have been my job since I am the Maid of Honor. But we all knew she would do a better job and knew exactly what my sister would love. Cassidy pulls out "TipsyLand," which looks like an adult version of CandyLand.

"Okay, y'all! Everyone, grab your drink of choice! We are playing TipsyLand!" Cassidy's slight drawl was always more pronounced when she drank. It's in full force tonight, and it's honestly adorable.

"Since I'm not drinking, I'll be a quiet observer," I say to Cassidy and Layla as the other women fill their drinks from the options provided.

"Boo, you whore," Cassidy replies.

"Mean Girls, really? How old are you?"

"Old enough to know what's good! But fine, don't play," she retorts before flouncing off to set up the game.

Layla peers at me and quietly asks, "You doin' okay?"

"Yeah, Sis. I'm good," I reply with a smile. "I don't mean to be a buzzkill. Seriously, I'll enjoy watching you guys make asses of yourselves."

"If you're sure...I bet most of us won't last much longer tonight," she laughs.

I get up while everyone is still getting situated and change into some comfortable leggings with a fitted tank top, sans bra. My hair is already pulled up in a messy bun, and I am ready to wind down. Once everyone else finds spots on the sitting room floor around the coffee table, I pull my legs up under me, criss-cross applesauce, and settle back into the couch to watch the train wreck I'm sure is coming.

***

Not long after the game starts, I feel a caress up the inside of my thigh. I startle and sit forward. It's as if someone was sitting next to me and leaned in to grab my leg. I feel a hand run from my bent knee almost to where it meets my hip. Dangerously close to my core.

Thinking I must be exhausted to be hallucinating sensual caresses, I shake my head and lean back into the couch. The game on the floor continues as if nothing happened, so I just keep watching as each woman gets progressively drunker and gigglier.

As the game is coming to an end and my sister is very close to passing out, I sit up with the intention of helping Layla to the bathroom to get ready for bed. But when I lean forward, I feel an unmistakable hand glide over my breast. My nipples instantly pebble against the touch. But then it's gone. My mind flits to the story of Patrick, the flirty ghost, but then I groan. *Seriously, I must be damned exhausted. There is no way I am being felt up by a ghost.*

"Layla. Let's get you ready for bed, yeah?" Ignoring the bizarre train of thought my mind just jumped on, I get Layla into the bathroom, helping her get changed and into bed. Not long after, all the other women are tucked into their beds, snoring quietly, sleeping off the impending hangovers. Deciding against using the pull-out mattress, I grab the blanket meant for the convertible bed, fluff the couch cushions, and curl up to go to sleep. I count my breaths to slow my heart and my mind, hoping sleep will take me soon. As I feel myself drifting off, I swear I feel a gentle brush of a hand over my cheek.

Chapter Two

I awake with a jump, as if pulled from sleep by a loud noise. But there is no sound, no commotion. In fact, as I look around the sitting room, everything is...*off*.

The colors are muted. The room is silent in a way that weighs on you. I look into the open door of the bedroom and see both beds empty. And then I realize the furniture isn't even the same. The bed frames are bulkier, with much more detail carved into the heavy wood. The bed spreads are heavy quilts that look nothing like the pristine white comforters I saw earlier. Turning back to the sitting room, it became clear to me that I was either dreaming or losing my mind. And honestly, it truly could go either way.

Below me, the cushiony couch is gone. In its place is a hard, settee style sofa. My blanket has disappeared. I look around, confused and disoriented. The TV stand is gone, replaced with an antique book-shelf. All the modern end tables are also gone. As I turn to look behind me, my gaze falls on a shadow in the corner by the door. I freeze, my body knowing that *fight and flight* aren't going to get me anywhere.

Slowly and deliberately, a man steps forward. He's young and handsome, probably in his early twenties. He has shaggy, light brown hair that falls against a clean shaven face. Even from a distance, I can see the freckles that coast over his nose and each cheek. He wears brown pants with a linen shirt tucked in and a matching vest, unbuttoned. My breath catches when he comes fully into the light of the moon that shines through the open window. He's the most gorgeous man I've ever seen. His build is strong and sturdy. It's clear that he's well toned under his clothes. His sleeves are rolled up, showcasing the lean muscles of his forearms and his large, calloused hands. My eyes finally make their way back up to meet his, and he smiles softly.

"Hello, Emery."

I gasp. "P-P-Patrick?" Somehow, I know. I just knew this is the man from the tour guide's story.

"I can't stay long, as you'll be waking up soon. But I wanted you to see me." He steps up to the back of the couch and leans over me slightly. "I see you, Emery. Come back to me." His hand reaches out, gently sliding the back of his knuckles across my cheek.

I'm stuck, unable to move. But I'm not even sure that I want to. My words catch in the back of my throat, but I don't know what to say even if I could speak. My mind is spinning and none of it makes any sense. When he realizes I'm not going to say anything else, he straightens and steps back. With a slight smile, he's gone.

Chapter Three

As I feel myself regaining consciousness, I squeeze my eyelids closed, unwilling to let go of the dream. I know, when I open my eyes, the hotel room will be the same as it had been when I laid down last night. And I'm not ready for it. That dream...Patrick...they have a grip on me that I can't explain. After a few moments spent trying to make sense of my feelings, I slowly open my eyes. I had cocooned myself in the blanket and the couch cushions as I slept. The sun filters through the sheer curtains on the window, which, I note, is no longer open. *Or maybe it never was? I don't even know.* I turn toward the bedroom and see all four women still soundly sleeping. Must be nice.

I stretch and slide out of the warm nest I had built in my sleep. Checking my phone, I notice it is still early, and since I am expecting the bride-to-be and her minions to sleep late, I decide to go on a quick run around the hotel grounds. Quietly, I grab my things and step into the bathroom. I quickly brush my teeth and change into yoga pants and a racerback tank with a built-in bra. I fix the mess that is my hair, securing it into a bun on the top of my head, and slide my shoes on. After grabbing my phone and AirPods, I slip out the door.

***

Depression is a fickle bitch. Sometimes the medication works like a dream, but then, like a sentient being, it figures out how to get around that barrier. I usually feel when a dip is coming and can combat it with exercise until my doctor can adjust my medication. Running started as a desperate attempt to "run away from the monster that lived in my mind." *Thank you to my first therapist, who made me afraid of my own brain when I was a child.* And while that is still the basic idea, running became the safe haven. The sounds of my feet hitting the ground and the world turning around me usually serve to quiet my mind, just a little.

This morning, no amount of outside noise can quiet my deafening thoughts. I just keep replaying my dream. I keep seeing Patrick in front of me, out of the corner of my eye, behind my closed eyelids. Everywhere I look—*or don't look*—he's there. The dream was so vivid, so real. And I wish I had been able to react better to what I was seeing. I don't know why, but I feel a pain in my chest at the idea that I will never see Patrick again.

***

I'm pulling my AirPods out of my ears as I walk in the door of the hotel room. I can hear surprisingly animated chatter coming from inside the bedroom.

"Emery! Where were you?" Layla doesn't look too hungover, though her eyes look tired.

"I got up early and went for a run. I wasn't expecting you guys to get up for a while. How are you feeling?"

She rolls her eyes at me. "I'm fine, Emery. I am a grown woman, and I can handle the after-effects of alcohol." She pauses, and then with a smile, adds, "But thanks for putting me to bed last night."

"Anytime, Baby Sis."

"We are almost ready to head down for breakfast. Are you joining?"

"Go ahead without me. I need to take a quick shower, and I'll meet you down there."

She shrugs and walks over to Cassidy, doing her best to push the other women along. "Come on, bitches! I'm hungry, and as the bride, I should NOT be kept waiting!" She sing-songs the last word as she dramatically flounces her hair and strikes a sassy pose. Now it's my turn to roll my eyes as I turn and head for the bathroom.

I start the water, letting it warm up as I strip off my clothes. Right before I step in, I hear the faint sound of the main door latching as the bridal party makes their way out into the hall. The suite bathroom has a standing shower with a clear glass door. I pull it closed as I step in and let the hot water run over my head and back. Now, in the quiet of the shower, my mind drifts back to Patrick. *Was it real? Could it be? Was it him I felt while the tipsy CandyLand was going on?*

I finally open my eyes and grab the washcloth and body wash. I quickly wash my body, use the bar soap over my face, and am rinsing my hair of shampoo when the air around me starts to feel...off. The temperature of the shower is changing. Not the water, the shower itself. The water is still hot. But the steam disappears from around me, and the condensation on the glass door fades until it's crystal clear.

Outside of the hot stream of water, the air in the shower is freezing. *What in the world?*

I stand still for a second, waiting to see if an explanation to this phenomenon randomly appears. But as I wait, I suddenly feel him. He's here. In the shower with me. I feel the weight of a person behind me, but since I'm facing the door of the shower, I can clearly see the mirror. No one is there.

My breath catches as I feel a featherlight touch skim up my side, landing on the side of my breast. The touch is faint as it flits across my nipples and down my other side. I close my eyes, my breath hitching. My heart is pounding, and I'm afraid to move or say anything, lest this sensation stop. The phantom hands continue down to cup the curve of my ass before slipping in between my legs from behind. I arch my back instinctively, yearning for the attention my body is receiving.

All of a sudden, the steam is back, swirling around me, making me lightheaded. But I still feel the weight at my back, the gentle caress of fingers between my legs. *Why does this feel so good?* Normally, I need direct stimulation to the clit to even consider coming. And yet, just the barest grazes through my folds and around my entrance are building my climax faster than I can anticipate.

My breathing is coming faster now, my chest heaving, as I feel a second hand return to my peaked nipples. Light caresses across each one, paired with the constant ministrations at my core, have me crying out. I reach back to grab my invisible suitor, but nothing is there. Instead, I tip forward to find purchase on the shower wall, afraid my knees will buckle. The unexplainable weight feels like it's following me. The ghostly set of hands continue their travels. And I shatter as the most intense orgasm I've ever felt rips through my body.

The phantom hands guide me all the way through my climax while helping to lower me to the shower floor, as my knees do indeed buckle.

Once I come down from the high, his presence disappears. The water starts to run cold from the amount of time I've spent in the shower. I quickly turn it off and step out, leaning back against the vanity as I continue to regulate my heart rate and breathing.

What the fuck was that?!

***

After I get dressed and make myself presentable enough to meet the ladies downstairs for breakfast, I open the door to leave the hotel room. Before I can step out, I feel a set of lips meet my ear and quietly whisper, "Come back to me." I shiver as I step into the hallway and shut the door.

CHAPTER FOUR

By the time I get home from the Lunar Hotel that afternoon, my mind is entirely wrapped up in Patrick. I didn't tell Layla what happened at the bachelorette party. She would think I was having some sort of a breakdown, and she didn't need that stress right on the verge of her wedding. So, the entire drive home was spent silently mulling over each interaction with him. What did they mean? Were they even *real?* Was I crazy? That last question was serious. I already couldn't trust my mind 100% of the time. Had I finally lost it completely? No, I can't start spiraling.

To combat these persistent questions, I decide to do the most healthy thing I can think of: get a Tinder date. Okay, yeah, not super healthy. But I need to get Patrick out of my mind, and I figure the best way to do that would be to have someone else's touch erase his. A *real* person's touch.

I unpack my overnight bag, tossing everything into the laundry to do later. I flop down on my oversized couch, sinking into the worn cushions, and pull up the Tinder app on my phone. It takes a bit of swiping left before I find a profile worth considering.

The guy, Theo, seems fairly normal. His profile pic is of him outside, in front of a tree. He has sunglasses on, so I can't see his eyes, but he has a nice smile. His hair is a dirty blonde with a matching, trimmed beard. He's wearing a maroon shirt with nothing on the front and dark jeans. No apparent red flags. I swipe right and set my phone down, getting up to get myself a bottle of water.

When I sit back down, my phone vibrates with a message from Theo.

> Hey :)

I had a tried and true system when it came to utilizing Tinder for hookups, so I cut right to the chase.

> Hey. So, in the interest of saving time, I am only interested in one thing here. Intrigued?

> Very. Continue.

> I am willing to give you my address if you are willing to send me a copy of your photo ID. I will send it to my sister so she knows who I am with and you can come over and fuck me. Sound good?

> Hold please.

A minute later, I get another message showing a clear picture of his photo ID. I shoot back my address and ask when I can expect him.

> Walking out the door as we speak. GPS says I'm 15 minutes away.

Wonderful. I forward the image of his ID to Layla and get up, heading for the bathroom to freshen up. I do a quick walk through of my house just to make sure everything is presentable before going back to my living room and grabbing my phone. Layla texted me back.

> Seriously?? You've been home like, 5 minutes!!

> The pussy wants what the pussy wants.

> That's not how the saying goes…

> Well, using the "heart" doesn't fit in this context sooooo…

> God, sometimes I wish I could swap places with you. Even single I couldn't sleep around like you do. (NOT shaming you.)

> Whatever, have fun. Be safe. Make good choices. (Imagine my best Jamie Lee Curtis from Freaky Friday there.)

> You're such a fun sucker ;) Love you.

> Haha. Love you too.

I'm closing out of my text thread with Layla when the doorbell rings. I open the door to reveal Theo. All 6 feet and some inches of him. *Damn.* The real-life version of him is much better than the picture, and the picture was pretty damn good.

"Hi. Emery?" he asks with a smile.

"Yeah. Hi, Theo. Come in." I step aside to let him in and close the door behind him.

"Your home is beautiful. You have a great neighborhood too."

"Thanks," I reply. "It's quiet, so it suits me." I offer him a drink and invite him to sit while I get our waters. Instead of sitting in the living room, he follows me to the kitchen, taking a seat at my bar. I slide the ice water across the counter to him and stand there, sipping mine.

"So, I know you only want one thing, but can we talk for a bit? I need to know you a little before we just jump into bed." Since I am standing while he is sitting, he looks up at me from under long lashes.

"Of course. I would never expect someone to do anything they're uncomfortable with."

He breathes a sigh of relief. "Cool." He offers me a dimpled smile before starting in.

***

The conversation flows easily between us. Theo really is wonderful. I find myself laughing and smiling as we banter back and forth. Before we realize it, the sun has gone down and the sky outside my window has grown dark. We've moved from the kitchen to the living room. There's a natural pause in the conversation, and I lean into him as we sit side by side. He wraps his arm around me and leans in to kiss me. But he pauses right before his lips meet mine, silently asking for permission. I lean forward and close the space between us. His lips are soft, and I part mine, allowing his tongue to slip inside. He's slow and methodical, savoring the taste of my mouth. It's nice, but I need more.

Without breaking our kiss, I move to straddle him on the couch. His head leans slightly back as I push my tongue a little more fervently against his, trying to heat things up. His hands move to my waist as I settle onto his lap. Immediately, I feel his hardness between us. I adjust so it fits right where I need to feel it through my leggings. I start to move, grinding down on him gently. His hands slip to my hips, tightening as he helps guide me. Our kiss breaks as we each pant into each other's mouths. I move faster and faster until he forces me to stop.

"Fuck," he speaks through gritted teeth. "I need you out of these clothes." His voice is growly with lust as he stands up, holding onto the back of my thighs so that I stay against him. My ankles cross behind his back, and my arms wrap around his neck as he walks me from the living room to the bedroom. He taps a quick kiss to my lips as he sets me on the edge of the bed. Grabbing the hem of my shirt, he pulls it over my head and tosses it on the floor. Quickly, he unhooks my bra and throws that aside too. His eyes trail down my naked torso, and he reaches out to cup both breasts in his hands.

"Fuck, you're beautiful."

My back arches, and he twists my nipples between his fingers before bending down and taking one nipple into his mouth. His tongue draws circles around one as he tweaks the other with his fingers, switching to ensure they get equal attention. Slowly, he begins kissing down my stomach, easing me back but giving me enough time to stop him if I am uncomfortable. I don't stop him. I need this. I lay back on the bed as he pulls my leggings and panties down my legs. He grabs my hips and yanks me to the very edge so my ass is almost falling off. He lowers himself to his knees so he's eye level with my clenching center. Slipping my legs over both of his shoulders, he lets my thighs fall open.

"Jesus, I can already see how wet you are. Is this all for me, baby?"

I moan as his words light a fire in my core. His hands slide up my inner thighs, and he slips a single finger inside.

"You're so tight. So warm." He dips in further, rotating his finger as he crooks it at the knuckle. My hips buck, and he chuckles. He slides a second finger in, and then I feel his breath against my clit. "You're so ready for me, baby. Such a good girl." Then his mouth clamps over that tiny bundle of nerves, sucking hard. I jerk against his mouth and cry out in pleasure. Grabbing his head, I thread my fingers through his hair, holding him right where I need him.

"Oh my god, yes. Please!"

He moans around my clit, and the vibrations add to the intensity of the pleasure. I'm so close. I can feel my orgasm cresting.

"Come for me," he whispers as he nips my clit with his teeth.

That should have done it. That last bit of pressure. But those words are like a bucket of cold water being poured over my head. My orgasm dies just as quickly as it built, and my body goes rigid. All I can hear is the ghostly voice of Patrick whispering, *Come back to me.* Tears well in my eyes from frustration. *This cannot be happening.* Theo notices the change in me and sits up.

"Hey, hey. It's okay. We can stop. I'm sorry."

"Jesus, you're being so understanding. I'm the one who is sorry. You did absolutely nothing wrong. In fact, it was amazing. I don't know what is going on with me." I groan and put the heels of my hands into my eyes, my face heating with embarrassment.

"Seriously, it's okay." He grabs the throw blanket that was draped over the armchair in the corner of my room and gently wraps it around me, pulling me into a sitting position. "Do you want me to stay?"

"I think I need some time alone to figure my shit out. I am so sorry for wasting your time."

"Hey, stop." He pulls my hands from my face and tips my chin to look at him. "I had a great time tonight, regardless of how it ended. If you ever want to hang out again, I'd love to, even if we just talk. I've enjoyed getting to know you."

I smile sheepishly at him. "I'd like that." I wrap the blanket tighter around myself and stand. We walk to the front door, and he presses a kiss to my temple before stepping out and closing the door behind him. I flip the deadbolt and head back to my bedroom.

Tossing the blanket to the floor, I go to the bathroom and start the shower. Before I can second guess myself, I step in and try to recreate the feelings in the hotel shower. I skim my hands softly over my body. With my eyes closed, I picture Patrick as I had seen him in my dream. He's behind me, his erection pressing into my ass. His hands slide down my belly to the warm center between my thighs. I imagine calloused fingers parting my folds and slipping into my wet cunt. The heel of that calloused hand presses against my clit, and I hitch a breath as I feel my orgasm building. Just a few strokes from my own fingers and the press of my hand to my clit has me crying out in my release. It's nothing close to the experience I had in the hotel shower, but it was all I could manage. I had needed *him*. But he isn't here. He isn't *real*. And I am fucked.

CHAPTER FIVE

T he next week seems to slowly crawl by. All I can think about is Patrick. My dreams consist of replays of each encounter I've had with him. I desperately wish I had more to play through.

Theo and I start texting fairly regularly, and it's nice, but I can't help feeling like I'm not being fair to him. Clearly, my mind is with someone else, regardless of how ludicrous that is. But I enjoy talking to him, and he's never pushed for another hang, so I try not to overthink it.

After waking up on a Wednesday morning, wet between my legs from another dream about Patrick in the shower, I decide I need to do something about this obsession. I call the Lunar Hotel to see when that room is available. I know it's their most popular reservation, but I'm crossing my fingers that the middle of the week is not a popular time for that particular request. And what do you know? Crossing my fingers worked. That room is available tomorrow. Before I can convince myself it's crazy, I book it.

***

My heart starts racing as soon as I pull into the hotel's parking lot and keeps racing all through check-in. As I make my way to the room, I try to calm my heart rate through my breathing, but the anticipation is too high. I unlock the door and step in, remaining still for a moment as I take it all in. I'm not sure what I was expecting. It's not like I thought he'd be sitting on the couch waiting for me, but the emptiness in the room makes my stomach drop. *What if I made this all up in my mind? What if this trip is all for naught? What if I am a broken woman, and I never figure out how to fix myself?*

I walk into the bedroom and set my bag down on the bed farthest from the bathroom. I don't drink, but this occasion calls for some liquid courage. From a brown paper bag, I pull the bottle of wine I had purchased at a bodega and walk to the little kitchenette in the main room of the suite. I locate a glass and pour a generous amount after twisting off the cap. Taking a sip, I grab the bottle and head back to the bedroom. I pull out the Bluetooth speaker I brought, pair my phone to it, and start a calming playlist.

I continue sipping the wine even as I begin taking off my pants and shirt. Underneath, I wear a simple lingerie set—just a black lacy bra with matching thong. I set my wine on the bedside table and grab the vibrator I brought. It's my favorite one, the Satisfyer Pro 2. A lot of people like the clitoral stimulator shaped like a rose, but the Satisfyer Pro 2 has a handle, which makes it much easier for self-use. More *ergonomic*, if you will. I crawl up to the middle of the empty bed, close my eyes for a moment as if preparing for some major feat, and then lay back against the pillows.

I don't turn the vibrator on yet; instead, I let my hands travel over my body. Closing my eyes, I imagine a different set of hands. I palm my breasts then run my hands down my stomach and over my thighs, eliciting goosebumps everywhere. Reaching behind myself, I unhook my bra, slipping it off and discarding it on the floor. Blindly, I search for the vibrator on the comforter, and once I find it, I turn it on a low setting. I slide the vibrator under my panties and place the suction head over my clit, letting out a slight moan at the first sense of pleasure. Holding the vibrator with one hand, I use the other to continue softly roaming my body.

My skin starts to heat, my breath coming faster as my pleasure slowly builds. Deciding to kick it up a notch, I turn the setting up, causing my hips to buck off the mattress and another moan to slip past my lips. It's then that I hear a whispered, "Open your eyes."

My eyes fly open, but there's no one there. So I keep them open as I continue my process. But I start feeling gentle grazes that aren't from my own hands. My eyes fall closed again as I moan louder at the new sensations.

"Open your eyes, Emery. Let me see your soul."

I gasp and open my eyes again. I feel warm air, like parted lips skimming down my neck and over my breasts. Suddenly, my vibrator increases in intensity again, and an invisible weight presses my hand so the suction presses tighter over my clit.

"You came to me. Now come for me, Emery."

My vision goes white as my body seems to catch fire with the intensity of my orgasm. I can feel tears leaking from my eyes, and I babble nonsense as my body attempts to come back down. My vision slowly returns but that orgasm sapped all of my energy. As I'm passing into unconsciousness, I feel Patrick at my ear again as he whispers, "Sleep, Emery. I'll see you in your dreams."

CHAPTER SIX

I know I'm back in the dream version of the hotel room before I even open my eyes. The silence is thick and seems to hang in the air.

I'm still in the hotel bed, but the furniture is back to how it appeared in that first dream. Antique, bulky, with extravagant details carved into the wood. And sitting next to me in bed, casually leaning against the headboard is Patrick. He smiles down at me as I take in my surroundings.

"Hello, Emery," he whispers.

"Hello, Patrick." My voice comes out shaky and breathy.

"I wasn't sure if you'd ever come back."

"Neither was I." I lower my eyes. "I wasn't sure you were real. Are you? Real?"

He chuckles softly and slides down to lay next to me on the bed. We are both on our sides, facing each other, and he reaches over to caress my hip. "Do I feel real?"

Everything he's offered me has felt real. "Yes, but how is this possible? You died in the 1800s. Not sure if you know this, but it's 2025."

His smile grows. "I'm aware, Emery. And I am not sure how to explain what's happening. I've never been able to show myself to anyone before. But when you woke up in my reality, I knew you'd see me."

"Woke up in your reality? What does that mean?"

"This room always looks like this to me. Anytime they've changed it over the many years I've been here, I can see the changes made as they're happening but then it immediately reverts back to how it looked when I was alive. When you woke up and looked so confused about the state of the room, I knew you were seeing what I see. And so I knew you'd see me."

"Why me?" I ask shyly.

His smile falls a little and a tiny crease appears in between his brows. "I don't know. But I felt a pull from you from that first time you said my name, outside the hotel room that first night. And when you walked in, you seemed to have a light that filled you, directing me to you."

I can't help but snort. "A light. Yeah. Was it a black light?" I spit out sarcastically.

He frowns. "I don't understand."

I sigh. "I suffer from something called depression. I think you would have called it, like, hysteria? Or melancholia? But my brain works against me sometimes, and I feel a deep sadness. No one has ever used "light" to describe me."

Patrick gently grabs my face in both of his large hands. He tilts my chin gently to ensure I meet his eyes before whispering, "I see your light, Emery. It's deep in your soul, but it's there. And it calls to me." He closes his eyes and kisses my forehead before moving his hands to wrap around me. He pulls me into him, and I'm enveloped by his warmth. As I close my eyes and settle in, I know I could stay here forever.

***

"So, if my light draws you to me, what drew you to the other female guests throughout the years?" We've been deep in conversation for what feels like hours, and I finally muster the courage to ask him about his *reputation* as the flirty ghost.

He frowns at me, looking slightly confused. "I'm not sure I understand."

"Patrick, come on," I scoff. "Your room is the last stop on the ghost tour. They say it's the most popular room in the hotel because of the *flirty* ghost of the young stonemason. Your reputation precedes you." I say it all teasingly, but deep down, I need to know. How many other women has he entertained like this?

"Emery, darling, there's only been you." He's begging me with his eyes, and I can see the desperation of his sincerity.

Softly, I respond, "I believe you. But why is that story told if nothing has ever happened?"

He visibly relaxes and rolls to his back. Shrugging he says, "I've spent a long time here, Emery. I suppose I get bored, and when I am able to reach through the veil, I feel a little...tricky." He smirks and rolls his head to the side to look at me.

"Tricky?! And what, pray tell, is your definition of *tricky?*"

He looks alarmed by my response. "I play tricks! I tug on hair or make the curtains move when the windows aren't open. Sometimes, I've brushed my hand over shoulders or chuckled quietly. Anything to ease the monotony. But it can be difficult to push through the veil in your reality, so I don't try consistently."

The panic eases in my chest now that I know he really did just mean *tricky.* "You've pushed through for me quite a few times."

His face softens. "It's easier with you. It's like the veil knows who you are to me and eases my path to you. Though, it doesn't just stay open for me. I've wanted to be with you when you're awake too, but it's not as...direct...when you're awake. It's difficult to articulate. It's as if I have to wade through fog and, sometimes, by the time I get through, it's too late."

I tuck myself into his side. "So...I'm the only woman you've met in this dreamscape?" I can't bring myself to look in his eyes. I don't want him to see the insecurity in mine.

He kisses my forehead. "You're the only one, my darling. No one else could have woken here with me. Your light brought you here, brought you to me."

His words wash over me and make me feel a sudden warmth in my chest. Could this be love between us? And if it is, what does that mean for me?

***

I stay in that dream space with Patrick for as long as I can. We spend the night talking and learning about each other. We never stop touching. If we aren't cuddled up in the covers, we are gently tracing the contours of each other's bodies over the sheet. It never goes any further. It feels like we are under some sort of spell as the conversation flows and neither of us wants to break that spell. I need to know him, all of him. And as I feel morning coming, and my body starts stirring to wake, I begin to panic.

"I don't want to lose this. I don't want to lose you," I cry, frantically grabbing onto the front of his shirt.

"Shhhhh, it's alright." Patrick eases a stray piece of hair from my face and gently kisses my lips. "Keep coming back to me. Anytime you're here, you'll see me. I promise."

A weight sinks into the pit of my stomach. This is the only place I can access him. I can't hold on to him. This isn't feasible. Seeing the despair on my face, he pulls me tighter to him and kisses me deeply. The kiss seems to go on forever as I sink into the feeling of immense love that he seems to emanate. He pulls away first, and I gasp at the loss of his lips. Opening my eyes, I see that I'm awake in the modernized version of the room. Sun filters in through the window, and I burst into tears.

CHAPTER SEVEN

I take my time getting ready, lingering in the hotel room as long as I can before check-out, foregoing my morning run. I am desperately hoping to hear or feel something from Patrick. I'm not ready to leave him. Rationally, I know this has to be the last time I indulge in this fantasy. I can't keep coming back here. But emotionally, it's physically painful to imagine never seeing him or feeling him again. I am so torn, so confused.

When it becomes clear that I won't encounter him, I dejectedly grab my bag and head toward the door. With one last look around, I leave.

***

Returning home is worse this time around. The house is quiet, but not the weighty silence of my dreamy hotel room. Normally, I relish being alone and not having anyone else in my space. But now, I yearn for Patrick to pull me into his arms and integrate himself into my entire life.

I put on a classical music playlist so the empty silence isn't so oppressive as I unpack my bag. My mind is wandering back through my latest dream as I hear my phone vibrate on the table. Picking it up, I see Theo's name appear, indicating a new text from him.

> Hey, a friend of mine is having a party tonight. Wanna go with?

The last thing in the world I want to do is go to a party with a bunch of strangers, on the arm of someone other than Patrick.

> Meh, not really my thing. But thanks for the invite.

He doesn't text me back, and I settle into my evening by making some dinner and sitting myself down to watch some trash TV. Seriously, if people falling in love in separate pods doesn't keep my mind occupied, what will?

Shortly after 10pm, my phone starts ringing. It's Theo. *Who fucking calls anyone anymore??* Reluctantly, I answer the call.

"Theo?"

"Emeryyyy." His voice is heavy, and he drags my name out, unnecessarily.

I laugh. "Are you drunk, Theo?"

"Just a little. But I wish you were here," he trails off.

"Sorry, man. Parties aren't my thing. But it seems like you've had a fine time without me."

"Can I come over?" he asks abruptly.

I pause. Do I want him to come over? If he comes over, I know what he'll want to do. Am I ready for that? Do I want another man touching me? Would this be good for me or send me spiraling like last time?

"Em?"

"Sorry, uh. Yeah, Theo, you can come over. But don't drive."

"I'm gonna grab an Uber. I'm excited to see you." His voice drops lower on that last sentence, and it's very clear *why* he's excited to see me. My stomach clenches, but I ease out a breath.

"See you soon, Theo."

***

Twenty minutes later, Theo is swaggering through my front door. He's clearly intoxicated, but not as much as I expected from that phone call. Before we make it all the way into the living room, he pulls me into his arms, buries his head in my neck and inhales deeply. His voice is growly when he says, "I've been thinking about feeling you since I left that day."

I stiffen a little in his arms, unsure how to answer. After a beat, I say, "Let's get you some water, yeah?" I pull away and lead him into the kitchen.

Instead of sitting at the bar like he did last time, he follows me around to the sink as I fill his glass. He comes up behind me, pressing into me and wrapping his arms around my stomach. His head drops to my neck and starts leaving a trail of slow, open-mouthed kisses from my ear, down my neck to my shoulder. I freeze for a moment, and then make the deliberate choice to lean back into him and let him explore. I need something real. Something I can potentially keep. Maybe that's Theo.

He moves to the other side of my neck and grazes my earlobe with his teeth. He drags his teeth down my neck, and then licks his way back up. His hands start roaming over my waist and hips. A sultry sigh slips from my lips, and he takes it as an invitation to go further. His fingers toy with the waistband of my leggings until he slips underneath. He slowly slides his hand inside my panties, toying with my clit with one finger.

I gasp as my body zings with pleasure, and he presses his erection into my ass, growling into my ear. His finger circles my clit, building the anticipation before stopping and sliding lower to my center. Again, one finger slips inside to encounter the heat and wetness that's been building. "Jesus, my memory didn't do this justice," he whispers into my ear. He slips another finger inside, massaging my inner lining and eliciting a whimper from me. I close my eyes and fall into the sensations he's creating, as he grinds into my ass.

After a moment, his breathing gets heavier, and he stops abruptly, spinning me to face him. "I need to be inside you. I've needed it since the other day. Please."

I nod, and he turns me around to the bar, bending me over it. From behind, he slides my leggings and panties down my legs, helping me step all the way out of them. Standing upright, he slides his fingers back inside me as I flatten myself across the bar. I close my eyes, relishing the feel of the cool granite against my cheek.

Theo pulls his fingers out, and I hear his zipper being drawn down. A foil packet is ripped, and he tosses the trash onto the bar within my line of sight. A moment later, I feel the tip of his condom-covered cock brushing against my clit. I hiss out a breath as he groans. He slides his dick from my clit to my center, spreading my wetness as he does. Then I feel the tip slip inside. "God, you're so tight. Fuck." Slowly, he inches his way inside until I feel his pubic bone press against my ass. He groans again and stills, hovering over me as I adjust to his size. The stretch feels intense, but the fullness feels good.

He starts moving, thrusting easily into me as he holds my hips in place. His groans fill the air around us, and while the feel of him is pleasant, it doesn't feel *right*. I feel no building of pleasure, no impending orgasm. And I can't take my eyes off of the torn condom wrapper, as if its mere presence is taunting me. His thrusting becomes quicker and harder. My hip bones dig painfully into the counter. "I'm close, baby. But I want to feel you come on my cock." I press my eyes closed as I feel tears building. At one time, his words would have lit a fire in my body, but Patrick's intense silence and quiet moans reverberate in my mind.

Theo slips one hand between me and the counter top, finding my clit. He massages it quickly, putting just enough pressure for me to finally feel the building tension in my belly. Between his continued thrusts and his skilled fingers, the orgasm crests, washing over me as I just continue to stare at the discarded condom wrapper near my head. "Fuck, baby, your pussy is clenching me so goddamn tight." With that, Theo succumbs to his orgasm. As he hunches over my back, still inside me, I realize that tears are silently streaming down my face. I take the moment while his brain is still hazy to wipe my face dry.

He finally leans up, slowly slipping out of me. I lift myself off the countertop, grabbing my clothes off the floor and heading to the bathroom as he discards the used condom and puts his flaccid cock back inside his briefs. I hear the echo of his zipper as I slip inside the bathroom door.

***

Once in the bathroom, I lean back against the door, looking up to the ceiling as I try to keep the tears at bay. *That didn't fix me. Theo didn't fix me.* I stifle a sob as I realize that no one is going to fill the hole that Patrick has somehow carved into my soul. I step away from the door and clean myself up, getting redressed. I splash some water across my face and arrange my features into what I hope is a satisfactory smile.

I step out to see Theo leaning against the arm of my sofa. He smiles at me as I walk toward him. "That was great, babe." He reaches for me and pulls me close to him, kissing my mouth as I settle between his legs. "Do you want me to stay?" His words remind me of our last attempt at this, and I nearly start crying again.

I take a deep breath and smile softly at him. "I don't think so. I'm not an overnight person." He looks a little taken aback, so I tease him, "No cuddling allowed, big guy. Maybe next time." I go to step back, and he reluctantly releases me. I try to busy myself in the living room while he pulls up the Uber app to get a ride home. *Or back to the party, I guess. It's still fairly early.*

His Uber arrives quickly. As I let him out the front door, he stops and kisses my lips. "Text me tomorrow." I smile at him, and he retreats down the front walkway. I close the door knowing that my time with Theo has come to an end.

Upon reentering the kitchen, I see the torn condom wrapper still sitting on my kitchen bar. With shaking hands, I quickly grab it and toss it in the trash, trying to hide it among other discarded items so I can no longer see it. As I wash my hands, another wave of tears lets loose, and I let them flow freely. I dry my hands and sink to the kitchen floor, pulling my knees to my chest. My body is wracked with sobs as I bury my face in my knees, letting out all my confusion and heartache. *What is happening to me?*

CHAPTER EIGHT

Apparently, Thursday nights are the best nights to book Patrick's room. I've booked out the next four Thursdays. And even that doesn't seem enough.

As I am walking through the front doors of the Lunar Hotel, I pop a sleeping pill into my mouth and swallow with a swig of water. I need to see him, and the faster I fall asleep, the faster I can get to him. I check in and hurry to my room.

Upon entering, I throw my bag on the other bed, strip off my clothes, and slide into *our* bed. I close my eyes and attempt to calm my breathing as I wait for the sleeping pill to kick in.

***

I wake with a jolt, flinging open my eyes and viewing my surroundings. *Oh, thank God.* I'm in Patrick's version of the room, but he's not in bed next to me like he was last time. I start to slide out from under the covers when he steps through the bedroom door.

"Don't get up, Emery. I'm here."

I ignore his request and throw myself into his arms. Tears form, unbidden, in my eyes, and I try to blink them away but Patrick seems to know. He pulls away gently and grabs my face in both hands.

"Hey, it's alright. You're here. I'm here." He kisses my lips and pulls me back into a tight embrace. We just stand there for a long moment, as the tension in my body eases, and I melt into his hold. When he is satisfied that I'm relaxed, he leads us to the bed and sits down on the edge. "Are you well? What happened?" He tucks a strand of hair behind my ear as he looks at me with concern in his eyes.

"I don't want to talk about it right now. I just need you." I scoot back in the bed, settling against the pillows. "Take your clothes off."

He pauses, still looking at me with concern, but then he stands and starts to unbutton his shirt. He never breaks eye contact as he makes his way down the shirt, tugging it out of his pants once he gets to the last button. I get a peek at his tan torso before he opens it and lets the white linen slide down his wide shoulders. I hear the fabric hit the floor, but I am mesmerized by his physique. His shoulders are broad and toned. His sculpted pectorals lead to chiseled abs and a tapered waist, showcasing his lean build. There's a smattering of light hair across his chest, and I yearn to run my fingers through it.

I'm pulled from the sight of his upper body by his fingers traveling to his pants, as he begins to undo them and allow them to fall to the floor. I can see the outline of his cock through his long briefs, and it makes my breath hitch. My heart is beating erratically as he slowly starts to push his last article of clothing down his legs. He stands back to his full height, fully naked in front of me. His cock stands at attention, almost reaching his navel. Saliva pools in my mouth as I imagine what it will feel like inside of me.

My eyes meet his and see they've gone black with lust. I swallow, suddenly nervous, as he begins to crawl up the bed to meet me.

"You have no idea how much I've yearned for you. How much I've needed you since hearing your voice for the first time and then finally seeing you. It took all my self-control to hold back when we were last together. I won't hold back now."

"I don't want you to," I whisper back.

He sits back on his heels once he reaches me and places his hands on my knees. He slides his hands up the inside of my thighs. As he starts to part them he whispers, "Let me see you, Emery. Show me what is mine."

His words set me on fire. The notion of being his fills something in me that, until now, I hadn't realized was painfully empty. I allow him to part my legs, and I realize I'm already soaked. *He hasn't even touched me yet.* He wraps his hands around my upper thighs, at the crease of my hips, and pulls me down the bed towards him. He leans down onto his elbows, stretching his body down the bed. "I've wanted nothing more than to taste you. To worship you. To wring the pleasure from your body." As he speaks, he breathes against my center, causing me to whimper.

"Please, Patrick."

"Please, what? Tell me, Emery."

"Please touch me, taste me, worship me," I breathe.

"As you wish." And then his tongue is probing my center, dragging my wetness up to my clit where he pulls that tiny bud into his mouth. But he lets go and his tongue lathes my center again, before returning and sucking my clit. He repeats this a few times as my body heats, my skin flushing. Small moans escape my mouth as I tangle my fingers in his hair and tug. He groans against me and increases the pressure of his tongue. He slides a finger into my sopping center, massaging gently. I gasp, and he inserts another one. His tongue has been working my clit mercilessly, and when he curls his fingers inside, I detonate. My entire body spasms with the power of the orgasm pulsing through me as Patrick continues to work me throughout it.

My body comes back down, and he leans up from between my legs, kissing his way up my stomach to my breasts, up my neck, and finally kisses my lips. My taste on his tongue is the most arousing sensation I've experienced. His tongue explores my mouth while he settles between my legs, keeping himself propped up on one hand. His other hand roams over my left breast, tweaking my nipple and massaging. He breaks our kiss and starts placing open-mouthed kisses on my neck. "You are more perfect than I could have dreamed," he breathes against me. "You were made for me."

As he continues trailing his lips over my skin, he reaches in between us and slides his thick cock through my folds, offering the slightest pressure every time he reaches my clit. Then he places his engorged head at my entrance and begins sliding in. My body welcomes him, as if it were waiting my entire existence for this very moment. Once he's fully sheathed within me, we both exhale jagged breaths. He locks eyes with me. "Don't close me out. Keep those beautiful eyes open, Emery. Let me see you. Let me see your soul."

My heart aches with the level of love those words elicit. We hold eye contact as he begins to move inside me. His thrusts are slow at first but they get increasingly erratic as the intensity of our connection builds. It's almost too much, and I let a tear slip down my cheek. Patrick leans down to kiss it away. "I know, darling, I know."

I feel as if I am nearing the edge of a cliff, and once I go over, I know there's no coming back. Patrick's thrusts grow harder and faster. Moans are leaking from both of us as we speed towards our impending orgasms. "You're mine, Emery. Your body, your being, your mind, your pleasure. You're mine." With those words and one final thrust, we both launch over the cliff together.

***

We're tangled up in each other beneath the sheet, my fingers absently toying with his chest hair. It's been quiet for some time as we both process what we just felt. Finally, I break the silence by asking, "Twice you've asked me to let you see my soul. Why?"

His hand, which was stroking my shoulder, pauses. He thinks for a moment before answering. "That light that I see in you...it's brightest in your eyes. And when I see the brightest part of that light, it feels like I am peering into your very being." His hand returns to gently caressing my shoulder. "Now, may I ask why you were so upset earlier?"

I don't know how to explain this to him. I don't know how to explain it to myself. "I need you in a way that defies explanation. It's like we are tied together, and I've tried to cut the cord, but I can't. Without you, I'm suffering. But when I'm with you, I'm suffering because I know I can't have you forever."

He tenses, knowing I am right. And I curse myself for putting such a heavy weight on an otherwise perfect moment together.

"I don't want to think about me leaving. I'm sorry. I just want to enjoy the time I have with you." I lean up and pull his lips down to meet mine. We share a long, sensuous kiss before Patrick pulls away.

"You're going to wake up soon."

"I know."

"I don't want you to leave without knowing how I feel about you, Emery. I've never felt this with anyone, even during my lifetime. I'm sorry I've placed this burden on you."

"Shhhh. Don't say that. Your love is not a burden." I kiss him again, but then his lips are gone, and I am awake, under a pristine white hotel comforter, in a room that looks foreign to me. I heave a heavy sigh as I get up and start getting ready to check out.

Before I leave, I say out loud to the emptiness, "I'll see you in six days." I pause before adding, "I love you." I hurriedly leave the room, brushing the tears from my face as I head towards the lobby.

***

The following Thursday goes much the same. I popped the sleeping pill before I even left the house. Risky, yes, but I wanted to waste no time once I got in the hotel room.

My eyes pop open to see the faded colors of the old furniture. I roll over in bed to see him lying next to me. Before I can get a word out, his lips are crushed to mine and his body is hovering over me. He kisses me hard and deep, like he's punishing me. He breaks the kiss, and I gasp in a breath.

"Don't ever leave me on the tail of those words again, Emery."

"I don't...w-what?" I manage to stammer.

"I can't always communicate with you as quickly as I want to when you're awake. When you said you loved me, I tried to say it back, but I couldn't break through to you. You effectively silenced me when you stepped out the door," he explains.

I hold his face in my hands, brushing kisses across his cheeks and down to his lips. "I'm sorry. I won't silence you again."

"I love you, Emery. Your light is a beacon, always calling to me." He kisses me again, this time slow and sensuous, taking his time to devour me. My light may be a beacon for him, but his love is a siren song that has entered my mind, my heart, my veins. I can't break the spell. And I'm not sure I want to.

***

It's even harder to leave him that next morning, and I have to force myself out the door, but not before I hear him whisper against my ear, "I love you, Emery. Come back to me." After our initial heated exchange that night, we worshiped each other's bodies, and we spent the rest of the night being in love. We talked and laughed. We held each other and cried, wishing we weren't separated by time and space.

The days in between each visit get more and more difficult. I force myself through the motions.

Brush teeth. *Check.*

Shower. *Check...some days.*

Get dressed. *Check. Do leggings and sweatshirts count?*

Eat. *Check...sometimes.*

Run. *Yeah, no. No check.*

I return my sister's texts since her wedding is in a week, and I don't want to alert her to my spiral. Theo finally stopped texting me when he realized short answers and turned-down invitations were all I could offer him anymore. I do everything I can to keep moving forward. But each day I seem to get foggier, and the air gets heavier and harder to breathe. I can't sustain this. But I don't know how to stop it.

***

The third Thursday, we lay in bed together after a long bout of love making. His hand twirls my hair as I subtly inhale his scent, wishing I could bottle it up and take it with me. *I wish I could take* him *with me.*

"Layla's getting married tomorrow?"

"No, Saturday. Tomorrow is the rehearsal dinner," I reply absently.

He says something, but I miss it as my mind continues to fixate on his smell and the feel of his body under my hand. Why can't I have this in life? Why did the love of my life die long before I was ever born? Did the universe mess up? Were we supposed to be together but we weren't born into the same world? Is that why he's been here all this time? Was he waiting for me? All the unanswerable questions are swirling through my mind like a tornado, loudly drowning out everything else.

"Emery. Where did you go?" Patrick turns my face to his, staring hard into my eyes.

The tornado disappears and a sob wrenches from my throat. "The light dims so much when I'm not here, Patrick. I can't see it like you can, but I feel it. If I keep this up, the light will go out altogether."

His brows crease. "I don't know what to do here, darling. Tell me what to do, and I will do it." He brings my knuckles to his lips and kisses them.

A sad smile forms on my lips, "There is nothing you can do, my love. Just keep showing yourself to me when I'm here." I tuck my head into the crook of his shoulder.

He pets my hair and whispers, "Always."

CHAPTER NINE

The music is too loud. My dress is uncomfortable, but I can't quite pinpoint why. Everyone is laughing and enjoying themselves, as they should. This is a party and a celebration of love. And yet, I am counting down the moments until I can extricate myself without getting a *look* from my sister.

Layla's wedding went off without a hitch. She looked beautiful and her husband, Derek, cried tasteful tears as she walked down the aisle to him. She couldn't have written a better photographic moment.

The reception is currently in full swing and my already low well of energy is going to be bone dry very soon. I faked my way through my Maid-of-Honor speech, and Layla was so caught up staring into Derek's eyes that she didn't notice how little feeling there was behind it. There's little feeling behind anything for me anymore.

I look around the open room, watching all the couples laughing and kissing as they soak in the bliss that is newly minted love. Layla and Derek dance happily in the center, beaming at each other. I'm happy for her, truly I am. But I feel such an intense pain in my chest knowing I can't ever experience anything like this with Patrick. He exists only in that room, in my dreams. And I exist here, in a world that seems too bright for me.

I finally decide that enough time has passed that I should be able to leave the reception without causing an issue with Layla. As the current song is coming to an end, I weave through the people on the dance floor, making it to Layla right as the last note plays.

"Baby Sis, let me say goodbye," I call as I come up next to her and Derek.

"You're leaving? It's early!" She grabs my wrists, attempting to make me dance with her.

"I'm starting to hit my wall so that's my cue to call it a night and leave you party animals to it." She laughs and pulls me into a tight hug. I close my eyes and hold tight to her for a beat too long. "I love you, Layla. You make a beautiful bride. And I hope you have an incredible time on your honeymoon."

She pulls out of the hug, keeping hold of my hands. "I love you, too, Em. I'll text you when I get back so we can have dinner or something!"

"Sure thing." I pull out of her grip, wave at Derek, and head out of the venue.

***

I spend the next four days in a dark hole. This Thursday is the last one I've booked in Patrick's room at the Lunar Hotel. And I've decided it's going to be the last one I *ever* book.

Chapter Ten

I smile at the receptionist at the check-in desk as I take my key. I feel lighter than I have in weeks.

I enter the room, smiling brightly, hoping he can see me though I can't see him. Heading straight to our bed, I set the unopened letter on the bedside table. I don't bother taking off my clothes or pulling back the covers of the bed. I just lay right on top of the white, plush duvet. I take the nearly full bottle of sleeping pills from my hoodie pocket and unscrew the cap from my water bottle, taking a small sip. I tap about half the bottle of pills into one hand, toss them into my mouth, and down them with a gulp of water. Taking a few more drinks, I make sure they all went down. Then I bring the bottle of pills to my lips and tip the remainder of the contents in. Again, I swallow them with a gulp of water, setting my water bottle and the empty pill bottle on the table next to the envelope.

I settle back into the pillows, waiting for the pills to do their job. It isn't long before the room starts to blur at the edges. It becomes harder to breathe, and I can feel my heart slowing in my chest. My eyelids start to droop, and it becomes more and more difficult to reopen them when they close.

"Open your eyes, my darling."

Slowly I open my eyes, desperate for the voice I am hearing. Patrick lies next to me in bed, brushing my hair from my face.

"Patrick," I slur out.

"Come to me, Emery." He presses a kiss to my lips.

I smile and close my eyes as I whisper, "Stay with me?"

It's a long moment, as his lips gently ghost over each of my closed eyes. "Until the end."

Epilogue

The young couple lingered on the edge of the group as they reentered the lobby of the hotel.

"Alright, folks! That brings us to the end of the tour. Please don't forget to take the survey that will be emailed to you shortly. Any feedback helps!"

"Wait!" The young woman stepped forward. "What about your most popular room? I thought that was the last stop on the tour?"

The tour guide frowned. "I'm not sure what you mean. This is the last stop on the tour."

"I was here 4 years ago, and the last stop on the tour was a specific room. With a story about a flirty ghost. It was said to be the most popular room in the hotel." The woman paused for a moment. "Why aren't we going there?"

"Ah, yes, that room is no longer a part of the tour."

The young woman had gone still, the apparent fight in her slowly draining. Another tourist spoke up. "Why?"

"A tragedy occurred there, um, 4 years ago, actually. And we no longer include that room." His eyes flashed to the young woman.

Another tourist, extra curious now, leaned forward. "A tragedy? What happened?"

The young woman seemed to find herself, steeling her shoulders as she said, "A woman committed suicide. Took a bottle of sleeping pills and never woke up." Her voice wavered as she spoke, and the man with her stepped to her side, putting his hand on her shoulder. The ring that glinted on his finger indicated he was her husband.

"Lay, let's just go," he whispered in her ear.

The tour guide was peering strangely at the couple before finally quietly asking, "Did you know her?"

Avoiding the question, the young woman asked her own, "Do people still report activity in that room? Is it the same activity, or has it changed?" She seemed almost eager at the prospect.

Again, the tour guide furrowed his brow before answering, "No ghostly sightings or encounters have occurred since the tragic suicide of the young woman. That room has gone wholly quiet."

The man held tighter to the woman's shoulder as she just stood there. "Layla, honey, it's time to go."

Tears built in her eyes, and she seemed to deflate as she let out a long, low breath. But then she straightened her back, nodded at the man, and threaded her fingers with his. Together, they left behind the Lunar Hotel and the heavy memories it held in its walls.

Acknowledgements

Dude...What the actual fuck?! I wrote a book...I wrote a freaking book?! This doesn't even seem real right now.

Okay, but seriously, I feel like there are so many people I have to thank, so I'll just dive in and see how it goes. (Ha! That's what I did for this whole book-writing experience!)

First off, Caitlyn, who is my "Ghost Porn" person from the dedication. Literally, during a ghost tour with her then-13-year-old daughter, I leaned over in a group of people and whispered (not so quietly because I do NOT have a natural inside voice), "When we get to the car, remind me to tell you about my ghost porn idea." Without missing a beat, she just nodded her head and said okay. And in that car ride home, we workshopped the entire book. When I got home, I was able to type up the outline. (And then it only sat on my computer for a year before I started writing it...) But I digress. You're my best friend, and my life would be infinitely suckier without you. You have been my champion through this whole thing. You've hyped me up to myself, to other people. You bragged on me as an author before I even started this thing. Your love and support mean more to me than you'll ever know.

Second, I have to thank the then-13-year-old daughter, Paeson. Thank you for sitting in that car, listening to your mom and your yom talk about ghost porn, and only mildly making fun of us. But more importantly, thank you for giving me the ending. I had no idea how I was going to end this thing. I didn't want him to come back to life, or her to just live her life loving a ghost. I think you were joking when you initially blurted out, "She needs to die at the end!" But seriously, she did. And you were right. I couldn't have done this without you. I love you like you're my own, babe!

To my incredible husband, who supports literally every endeavor I embark upon. I need to buy 6 Christmas trees? He helps me put them up. I say I want to start narrating audiobooks (but never do)? He says he will help me pick out the right equipment to buy. I say I want to read almost 300 books in a year? He lets me rant, rave, and cry to him about each and every book, having no idea what I'm talking about each time. I say I am going to write a ghost porn book? He asks if he's going to get to read it when I'm finished. Chad, I could not and would not do life without you. Thank you for being the opposite side of my coin. The quiet to my loud. The calm to my intense.

Mom. I love you more than my luggage. Thank you for being excited about this with me. Thank you for being the first one to read any of it. Thank you for always being proud of me and believing in me. Not related to this book, thanks for the hours-long phone calls we have, even though we no longer live across the country from each other and can see each other whenever we want. I love those phone calls more than you know. And thank you for allowing me to form such an amazing, open, honest relationship with you as an adult. You were my first best friend, and you taught me what female friendships should look like as an adult. That was one of the greatest gifts you could ever give me. Thank you.

BLT, thank you for suffering through, not just a hetero story, but a ghost hetero story with a questionably happy ending. Your friendship and support mean so much to me.

Kalie, I wish I could write this entire paragraph in movie quotes like I did my speech at your wedding. But I am drawing a blank. I need you to be here to pull the right quotes out. Thank you for reading this and giving honest feedback. As the one friend of mine who doesn't read romance, your perspective was much needed. More importantly, thank you for being my one true soulmate. We've been together since we were 11 years old, and we've changed a lot (and yet not a lot) in all these years. My life would not be whole without you. We never say it, but I am going to say it now, I love you.

Kayla, thank you for hyping me from the start! Thank you for being one of the very first preorders of this book. Thank you for designing my business cards in the middle of a busy Bedpost event. We've been friends for over a decade, and it's been amazing to support your small business ventures (also expensive because I can't stop buying your stuff). And words can't explain how much I appreciate your help, support, and guidance in this little adventure.

Izzy Elliott, DJ Aubuchon, and Annie Lisenby, if you made it this far, THANK YOU! Thank you for answering my never-ending questions, and responding to my emails and Insta messages. Thank you for liking all my lame Instagram posts. Just, thank you! This book could not have been published without your help.

To the incredible patrons of Bedpost Books—all of the vendors who not only sell their wares there but also shop there, all the customers who come in week after week—thank you! Thank you for supporting such an incredible small, local business. And thank you for helping to build this amazing community around us. I wouldn't have finally sat down and started writing this book without all of you and the support you show us and each other every single time you're there. You've helped make Caitlyn's dream come true, and in doing so, you've made my dream come true.

To all the people who beta read this and helped get it to its final version, thank you!!! Your feedback was instrumental in getting it to this stage. I hope I will have another book for you to beta read soon. ;)

And finally, to everyone who doesn't know me personally who picked up this little book and gave it a read, thank you. Thank you so much. You've made my dream of being an author come true by taking a chance on a first-time writer with a ridiculous story. Your support can never be repaid, but please know it means the world to me.

P.S. To all the paranormal romance authors out there, thank you for championing this genre and letting a book like mine even be possible.

About the author

Lola B. Marie was born and raised in the Midwest. She's an avid Chiefs fan, a terribly competitive fantasy football player, and a romance reader. She lives with her husband, son, dogs, and cat. All the pets are boys, and she doesn't mind being outnumbered. When she isn't reading, writing or with her family, you can find her hanging at Bedpost Books, her favorite locally-owned bookstore in the Midwest. She's also usually listening to one of a hundred podcasts while drinking Dr. Pepper and eating some sort of gummy candy.

As a typical pissy Pisces, she's also a dreamer who never expected one of her dreams to come true. Writing was always something she enjoyed, but she never thought she'd write something to completion.

And now she's a published author. Live your dreams, kids. They're possible if you want them to be.